MW00886391

VINTAGE ROSE MYSTERIES

NEW PAINTING

EVAN JACOBS

VINTAGE ROSE
MYSTERIES

The Secret Room

New Painting

Lucky Me

Call Waiting

VCR from Beyond

SADDLEBACK
EDUCATIONAL PUBLISHING
www.sdlback.com

Copyright © 2020 by Saddleback Educational Publishing
All rights reserved. No part of this book may be reproduced in any form or by any means, electronic or mechanical, including photocopying, recording, scanning, or by any information storage and retrieval system, without the written permission of the publisher. SADDLEBACK EDUCATIONAL PUBLISHING and any associated logos are trademarks and/or registered trademarks of Saddleback Educational Publishing.

ISBN: 978-1-68021-761-2
eBook: 978-1-64598-068-1

Printed in Malaysia

24 23 22 21 20   1 2 3 4 5

THE HISTORY OF THE VINTAGE ROSE ANTIQUE SHOP

The story begins with a sorcerer named Ervin Legend. He had a talent for making money. While traveling, Ervin bought items all over the world. He would have called himself a collector. Others might say hoarder. Once he grew tired of things, he sold them for a profit. "One man's junk is another man's treasure," he used to say.

Eventually, Ervin wanted to settle down. His home was in Scarecrow, California. But he needed somewhere to put all of his things. Ervin opened the Vintage Rose Antique Shop in 1912. It was a place to keep his collections. His wife, Visalia, inspired the shop's name. She loved roses and kept them in vases all over the shop. "Roses mask the smell of old things," she would say.

After the shop opened, Ervin kept traveling. He collected pieces to sell from all over. In 1949, Ervin and Visalia went to Cairo, Egypt. While there, the couple disappeared. Nobody knows what happened to them. Some say Ervin's love of sorcery might have been to blame. He may have looked into something he shouldn't have.

Family members took over the shop. None were quite like Ervin, though. Without his passion, the business began to fail. His sister believed it was cursed.

In 1979, the Legends put the shop up for sale. Rose Myers bought it. She was odd, like Ervin. Her passion for old things was like his. "Everything has a story," she would say, with a twinkle in her eye. From a young age, Rose had looked for bargains. She would resell things for a profit. Buying the Vintage Rose was her dream come true. The place was old. It was filled with odd treasures. Plus, Rose was part of the name of the store. It seemed like this was meant to be.

Rose ran the shop for 40 years. When she passed away, it closed. The business had been left to her nephew, Evan Stewart. He was Rose's closest living relative. The Stewart family moved to Scarecrow. They reopened the shop in 2019.

Today, the shop still holds many treasures. Collectors come from all over. Some have purchased these mysterious relics. Are they magical? Do they watch over the store? We may never find out. Or will we?

CHAPTER 1

THE GIFT

Come on, Tabitha," Heather says. "Just rip it open!"

"Yeah, Tab," Sasha says. "At this rate, you'll be 14 by the time you open that!"

Everybody at my 13th birthday party laughs. So do I. But that doesn't stop me from taking my time to open my last gift. Heather and Sasha don't care what it is anyway. They both stare at their phones. That's usually what they're doing.

Heather and Sasha are eighth graders. I'm only in seventh. The three of us don't hang out at school. We just live near each other, and our parents are friends. Our neighborhood is behind Scarecrow Middle School.

The last gift is big and flat. It's wrapped in beautiful orange paper. First I open the card. My cousin Denise wrote in it. She smiles at me shyly and adjusts her thick glasses. Denise doesn't really know anyone at the party since she goes to a different school. But we have a lot in common. Both of us love art.

All eyes are on me as I start to tear the paper. My mom is taking pictures. When the wrapping comes off, my heart begins to race. It's a painting. Is this what I think it is?

Denise points to the artist's name at the bottom of the canvas. It's written in cursive with silver paint.

"An Ophelia Wretch?" I shout. My face bursts into a smile. I can't believe it!

"I know she's your favorite painter," Denise says softly.

"Thank you so much!" I give her a big hug. She seems surprised.

For a moment, we all stare at the painting. The subject is a strange-looking orange man with brown hair. His suit is gray. He doesn't have a nose or eyes. There are just empty, black sockets where those should be. A dark, shadowy background frames the man. I can tell the paint is faded. It makes me wonder how old this piece is.

"Where did you get it?" I ask Denise. "This is my first real Ophelia Wretch painting. They are so hard to find now! Collectors always snap them up."

"My mom found it at the Vintage Rose Antique Shop," Denise says.

"Oh, really? That's in Scarecrow." Denise and

her parents live in Sunnyside. It's the next town over from Scarecrow. I wonder what they were doing at the Vintage Rose.

"Yeah. She bought it during their grand reopening a while back."

My aunt walks over from where she was standing with my mom.

"Hi, Aunt Becky! Thank you so much for the painting. How did you find it?"

"Oh, you're very welcome. It was just something I picked up while browsing the Vintage Rose. That's such an interesting shop."

I nod. *Interesting* is one way to describe the Vintage Rose. There's all kinds of weird stuff in that place. Sometimes kids from my school go there to mess around. They grab free items from the pass-along section. This is a part of the store where people donate things, and anyone can take them for free. As kids, my brother and I went to the store a few times to look for Halloween costume accessories. I haven't been there in years though.

Aunt Becky goes on. "When I brought the painting home, Denise recognized the artist. She said you loved her work. It has been in a closet ever since. We've just been waiting for your birthday!"

My aunt goes back to chatting with my mom. The party is starting to break up. Some of my friends are glued to their phones. It's clear they're ready to go. I should say goodbye to them. But I'm not done looking at the painting yet.

My best friends, Steven and Kendra, walk up. "You actually like that?" Steven asks. "Isn't it a little . . . dark?"

I laugh. Steven always wears button-down shirts in bright colors. He would never dress in a gray suit like the orange man.

"It's awesome!" I say. "Look at the lines and shadows. The way the colors contrast is so unique."

"It's cool," Kendra says. She smiles a bit. "If you're into creepy things."

The two of them laugh.

"Maybe it's a little odd," I say. "But it's an Ophelia Wretch! She's my favorite artist. Her paintings are so vivid. They really make you think. Did you guys know she's from Sunnyside?"

"No," Steven says. "Maybe you should go visit her. You two could have a painting party." He grins.

I frown. "Too bad she died in the 1980s, or else I would."

"Oh, sorry," Steven says, looking down.

All of my friends know I love to paint. But they

don't always get how passionate I am about it. My paintings are on almost every wall of our house. Most of them have girls as the subjects. That's my thing for now. Someday I hope to be like Ophelia Wretch. She is known around the world for her unique paintings. Since we're from the same area, I think of her as my painting soulmate.

"You're not planning to keep that, are you?" Heather asks. She looks up from her phone and scowls at the orange man.

"Of course I am. It's going up in my room immediately."

"No way," Sasha says. She scowls too.

Why did my mom even make me invite these girls to my party? We have nothing in common.

"That painting is mega-weird," my brother chimes in. Doug is at least a foot taller than all of us. He plays basketball at Scarecrow High School. Because he's so tall, everything he says seems to float through the room.

"Shh," I say. "Denise and Aunt Becky might hear you."

"Whatever."

Doug walks away. He goes over to the cupcakes and picks up three of them. Then he shoves them in his mouth.

Steven and Kendra crack up. I just roll my eyes.

At least Heather and Sasha will go home soon. I'm stuck with my brother forever.

CHAPTER 2

TRUE COLORS FADING

I nudge the painting of the orange man a little to the left. Now it's perfectly centered on the wall across from my bed. An old painting of mine had to be moved first. But it only seemed right to make the Ophelia Wretch painting the centerpiece of my room.

After admiring it for a moment, I pull out my phone. Once I've found the best lighting, I take a picture of the painting. This is going on my Instagram. The caption says, "New Ophelia Wretch from Cousin Denise." I add a heart emoji and a few hashtags before posting it.

There's a real Ophelia Wretch piece in my room. I still can't believe it. Some of my paintings hang on the other walls. There are also pictures of me, Steven, and Kendra tacked up. We've been best friends since fourth grade.

My easel stands in front of the orange man. There's a half-painted canvas on it. This is a new painting I'm doing. It features a rowboat on a lake. A girl leans over

7

the side of the boat. She dangles her hand in the water. You can't see her face at all. The sun is coming up in the background. Across the lake is an old log cabin.

I stare at the painting of the orange man. For some reason, his orange skin looks more faded now. His black hair appears grayer too. Maybe it always looked like this. The lighting is different downstairs. It's brighter in my room. That helps me when I'm painting.

My mom peeks her head into my room. "You already hung that up?" she asks.

"Of course!" I answer. "Mom, you know I love Ophelia Wretch."

As she walks into my room, Mom stares at the painting. She almost seems mesmerized.

"For something you think is weird, you're sure into it," I say, laughing.

"It's so eerie, Tabitha," Mom says. She looks at me now. "Even without eyes, the man seems to be looking at us."

"Really? I hadn't noticed."

I move around the room. The empty eye sockets don't seem to follow me. My mom is just being silly.

"It's not looking at Tabitha," Doug says. He stands in the doorway now. There's a big smile on his face. "Even without eyes, that guy doesn't want to look at her!"

My brother laughs and walks away.

Mom just shakes her head. I think about saying something back to him. Then I get a text. It's a group chat with Steven and Kendra.

Steven

movies?

Kendra

cool. what 2 see?
scary movie!

It's Sunday. My parents don't usually let me go out on school nights.

"Mom," I say. "Can I go to the movies with Steven and Kendra? I know there's school tomorrow, but it's still my birthday."

She knows how much I love the movies. "Okay," Mom says.

This birthday keeps getting better!

CHAPTER 3

NO EYES ON ME

Steven and Kendra took me to see a zombie film. It was fun. Kendra loves scary movies. Steven and I think they're funny. We don't get scared easily.

Now I'm home and getting ready for bed. I turn the light off in my room and climb under the covers. It's hard to sleep though. The excitement from my birthday hasn't worn off yet.

This was a big day. I'm finally a teenager. Everyone told me not to be in a hurry to grow up. I loved being a kid. But being a teenager is going to be so much better.

High school is just around the corner. That means I'll be able to take a bunch of art classes. My plan is to study art in college.

Dad always says, "Tabitha, you're going to need something to fall back on. Artists don't make a lot of money. You have to be really famous. Even then, fame doesn't last forever."

Right now, none of that concerns me. Someday I

will have to think about it. But I'm still holding onto my dream.

I close my eyes. There's school tomorrow. Sleep is important. My brain doesn't want to shut off though.

When I open my eyes again, they're drawn to the painting. Moonlight shines through my window. It hits the orange man just right. I can see his face perfectly.

Something about the painting startles me. My eyes are transfixed on it. Maybe Mom was right. The orange man looks like he's staring right at me. How can that be? He doesn't have eyes.

I get out of bed in the dark room. My eyes are still locked on the painting. Slowly, I shuffle closer to it. It's like the orange man is drawing me in.

Does he have me under a spell or something?

No, that's impossible. I'm just a big a fan of Ophelia Wretch. This painting is a bit weird. Still, I love it.

A few feet from the painting, I stop. The light of the moon illuminates the empty eye sockets. The closer I get, the less it looks like the orange man is staring at me.

Now I feel silly. The angle from my bed probably made the painting look strange. I've actually heard of this. People say the eyes of the *Mona Lisa* seem to follow you. It has to do with shadow, light, and perspective. Whatever it is, I'm just glad that the orange man isn't looking at me anymore.

My hand touches the canvas. This is a no-no. The oils in my skin can damage the paint. But I can't help it. It's like the orange man wants me to.

The paint feels thick under my fingers. It almost seems embossed. In the dark, it's as if the man is coming out of the canvas. His features appear 3D. Did the painting look like this before?

"Okay," I whisper to myself. "No more scary movies for a while."

I get back into bed. Being creeped out by a painting is silly. Besides, how many people own a real Ophelia Wretch? This thing could be worth a lot of money. None of that matters though. The painting is mine now. There's no way I'm selling it.

CHAPTER 4

BEING WATCHED

Even though I went to sleep late, I wake up early. My body feels refreshed. Usually getting up on Monday morning is hard. For some reason, it's easy today.

When I climb out of bed, my eyes are drawn to the painting of the orange man. It's much more vivid in the daylight. In the darkness, the eye sockets looked so haunting. I'm glad it doesn't seem to be staring at me anymore.

Since I'm up early, there's extra time before school starts. This is a good time to work on my own painting. I go to the easel and squeeze some blue paint onto my palette. There isn't much left. Maybe I can get some more tomorrow.

I start painting the background. This should be easy. There's not enough time to do anything too involved this morning. Quickly, I get into the zone.

A few minutes go by. Then I notice something. It feels like someone is watching me.

It's the orange man. He appears to be overseeing my work.

For a moment, the creeped-out feeling I had last night returns. But is it so bad to have someone watch me paint? This is probably how it's going to be in high school and college. Art teachers will observe my work. They'll give pointers. Some might be tough. The orange man could help me get used to this.

Mr. Zamora isn't tough at all. That's my art teacher at Scarecrow Middle School. He never hovers over his students. We tell him what we are going to work on. Then we show it to him when we're done. If we have questions, he's always willing to help. But most of the time our teacher gives us a lot of freedom.

After painting a bit more, I look up at the orange man again. He seems different now. His eye sockets look smaller. So does the area where his nose should be. These parts of the painting appear more filled in. Also, his skin isn't as orange. It looks more natural. Is it because the light from the window has gotten brighter? Maybe it's because I'm closer to the painting too.

"Are you planning on going to school today?" Mom asks. She pokes her head into my room. "I know you're a teenager now. Hopefully you aren't already starting to rebel."

"Yeah," I say, giggling. I'm still staring at the orange man. "Do you think the painting has changed since yesterday?"

"What?" Mom laughs. Then she comes into my room. For a moment, we both stare at the painting.

"Nope," she says with a smile. Mom knows how much I love art. I ask her weird questions like this all the time. "That man looks just as strange today as he did yesterday."

"Come on," I say. "You don't think the empty areas on his face look smaller? Or his skin tone seems brighter?"

"No." She begins to walk out of my room. "You're probably just excited about finally owning an Ophelia Wretch painting. And you've got the art competition this week."

That's right! How could I forget? The annual art competition is on Saturday. It's at the Scarecrow Public Library. I entered one of my paintings. A bunch of people from my art class entered pieces too.

This year's competition is special. The show is centered around Ophelia Wretch's paintings. Three of her most famous ones are going to be on display. They are *Man on a Bridge*, *Girl in the City*, and *Sailor at Sea*. For the next month, her paintings will be at the library. Then they'll move to another city.

I've been excited about the competition for months. Everyone who entered the contest gets to have their work on display next to Ophelia Wretch's. How cool is that? It will almost be like having a painting in a real museum!

"Tabitha, you had better get dressed," Mom shouts from down the hall. It snaps me out of my daydream.

I look at my painting. Somehow I accidentally painted part of the sun blue. My mind must have really wandered. There's no way to fix it now though. It's time to get ready for school.

CHAPTER 5

FRENEMY

Making that mistake in my painting threw me off all morning. I couldn't decide what to wear. My favorite cereal was all gone. Then there was a lot of traffic when Dad took me to school. It almost made me late.

How could I paint the sun blue? Thinking about the art competition distracted me. Still, it was almost like I wasn't controlling my hand when it happened. Had the orange man somehow made me do it?

That's impossible, I tell myself. A painting can't make me do things. The orange man might look odd, but he isn't real.

The day turned around after I got to school. Scarecrow Middle School is a big, white stone building with large windows. Two taller buildings sit behind it. One is a gym. The other is a multipurpose room. Outside, there's a track and a large field.

My good luck started with a quiz in language arts. I got an *A* without even studying. All day, people came up to wish me happy birthday. That was cool. At lunch, Kendra told the cafeteria workers I turned 13 the day before. They gave me extra chicken nuggets.

I have art and design during sixth period. This is my favorite class. Sometimes we paint. Other days we shoot photos or videos. Then there are days like today when we design projects on the computer.

Just as I'm logging in, my classmate Raphael walks up. He's wearing a bright yellow sweatshirt over a long-sleeved button-down shirt. This is how he usually dresses.

"I saw your Ophelia Wretch painting on Instagram," he says. "In a word—*creepy!*"

I roll my eyes. If I had to describe Raphael in one word, it would be *frenemy*. Both of us are into art. Aside from that, we're totally different.

For one thing, we treat people differently. I love giving encouragement. No matter how good or bad people are at something, I want them to do well. Raphael isn't like that. He never has anything good to say about anyone else. In art, he's always kissing up to Mr. Zamora. Getting praise is his goal. It makes him feel like he's better than everyone else. Whenever Mr. Zamora says something nice about my work, Raphael can't stand it.

Part of me just wants to ignore him. That would be rude though.

"Well, I love it," I say with a smile. Raphael shrugs and sits down at the computer directly across from me.

The project Mr. Zamora has assigned us is a poster. It can be for any movie or video game. We just have to make sure the poster is original. He wants us to do everything on the computer.

"Have you heard any news about the art competition?" Raphael asks. He doesn't look at me as he talks. Instead, he pretends to work on his computer. This is his way of making it seem like he doesn't care what my answer is. But I know he cares.

"No. Have you?" I don't look at him either.

Now I can feel his eyes on me.

"Um, no," he says.

"We won't hear anything until Saturday," Vincent chimes in. He's sitting next to Raphael.

"Guess we have to wait until then," I say.

It's clear that we all want to win. Raphael and I have a good chance, I think. The painting I submitted is of a cowgirl. She's riding a horse. Its front legs are raised as it rears up. Raphael's entry shows a bride in the rain. We ran into each other as we dropped off our paintings at the library. That was awkward.

Honestly, Raphael's is really good. He is very talented. I'm not going to tell him that though.

I focus on my poster. It's going to be for the video game *Clan Castles*. That's my favorite game ever. The goal is to defeat a dragon king named Nojra. Beating it is almost impossible, but that's sort of what makes it fun too.

"Nice use of color," Mr. Zamora says behind me. "I like how the title pops."

When I turn around, he's looking at my computer screen. "Thank you," I say, smiling.

Mr. Zamora moves around the room. Soon he's across from me.

"What do you think of mine, Mr. Z?" Raphael asks.

I briefly look up. Mr. Zamora stares at Raphael's screen.

"You're getting there," Mr. Zamora says. He rests a hand on his chin. "You just need to tie all your elements together. Keep at it."

I can practically hear Raphael deflate in his chair. He always expects compliments. Mr. Zamora doesn't always give them.

Part of me wants to laugh, but I don't. That would just be mean.

CHAPTER 6

EYES ON ME

Ugh," Steven says the next day. "I am so lost in math."

He, Kendra, and I are sitting at a booth inside the Golden Nugget. This is a chicken nugget place in Scarecrow Plaza. Their thick, melted cheese toast is my favorite. Kendra and I are sharing an order.

Scarecrow Plaza is the biggest strip mall in town. It's got an electronics store, a few clothing stores, a candy store, and a supermarket. There's also an art store called Bradley's that is my favorite. I could spend all day there.

"I can help you with math later," Kendra says to Steven.

We all hold our phones as we eat. Somehow we can talk while eating and checking our phones. I guess we're talented like that.

"Have you guys cleared any more levels in *Clan Castles*?" I ask.

"I keep dying on level 38," Steven says. "Maybe it's time to give up."

"That game was more fun when Scott Gomez was playing with me," Kendra says.

She has had a crush on Scott since fifth grade. Scott loves video games and skateboarding. Kendra started playing *Clan Castles* just because he talked about it all the time.

"You guys were playing together?" I ask. This is the first I'm hearing about it.

"Yeah, last week."

"Oh," I say. "Maybe he just got busy?"

"That was his excuse too." Kendra sighs and picks up another piece of cheese toast.

Scott Gomez has never paid much attention to Kendra. But she seems to get more obsessed with him every year. Next, she'll try skateboarding to impress him. I wish she would find a guy who likes the same stuff she does. Personally, I don't think about boys much. My art is more important to me right now.

After we finish our food, I go into Bradley's. The store is huge. They have paint, canvases, frames, brushes—any art supply you can think of, basically.

The walls of the store are decorated with paintings. Local artists display their work there. Maybe someday one of my paintings will be on the wall. I don't have anything good enough yet though. Still, my parents keep encouraging me to submit something.

Going to Bradley's is hard for me. I want to buy everything. Today I have to be quick too. My friends are waiting outside. Steven is still stressing over his math homework. He wants to get home so he can video chat with Kendra and get it done.

All I need today is some blue and white paint. Near the back of the store, I see a new painting. It shows a little boy in an amusement park. There is a Ferris wheel behind him. The gray sky is filled with big, gloomy clouds.

Then I take a closer look at the boy. He isn't smiling. And it seems like he's looking at me.

His eyes follow me around the store. Should I text my friends to tell them about this? They'll think I'm crazy.

Quickly, I search through the paint colors. Every time I glance at the little boy in the painting, his eyes are on me. It looks like he's scowling. The clouds in the painting seem to move behind him too. This is so disturbing!

I pay for my paint and leave Bradley's as fast as I can.

CHAPTER 7

FULL OF ITSELF

On our way home, I look in my bag from Bradley's. "Oh no! I forgot the white paint."

"Uh-oh," Kendra says. "What in the world will you do?"

Steven laughs.

"Yeah, real funny. I needed it for skin tones. How did I forget it?"

I can't believe my mistake. Yesterday I also messed up my painting. It isn't like me to make silly slipups like this. What's going on?

The orange man creeped me out. That painting of the boy in Bradley's scared me too. Art has never been scary to me before.

None of this makes sense. Paintings aren't alive. So why does it feel like they're watching me? Am I imagining things?

Later that night, I'm working on my history homework. There's a list of questions about Plymouth

Rock. I sit on my bed with my textbook next to me while writing my answers.

As I'm thinking about one question, I glance up at the painting of the orange man. My body freezes. The man's skin color looks even less orange now. It's fresher and more lifelike.

In fact, everything about the once-orange man looks more natural now. His nose and eye sockets are nearly filled in. The man's black hair and suit also look as if they've gotten a new coat of paint. He even seems to have shifted his position.

I get up off my bed and move toward the painting. Soon my face is inches from it.

A sharp twinge of fear shoots through my body.

Now I'm sure that the man's nose is more filled in. There's even an outline of what looks like a new nose forming.

How is this possible? It's like someone has painted my painting.

"What are you doing?" Doug asks. He's standing in the doorway. His arms are folded. "You look like you're going to kiss that creeper."

Turning to Doug, I narrow my eyes. "Have you been messing with my painting?"

"What?" He laughs loudly. "Why would I do that?"

"Because you hate me!"

"Not that much," Doug says. Then he walks away.

Part of me feels bad now. Nobody likes being blamed for something they didn't do. I believe my brother. He knows how much I love art. There's no way he'd actually paint on my Ophelia Wretch. Would he?

Maybe Mom or Dad did it. That seems even less likely, though.

Everybody's gone during the day. My brother and I are at school. Our parents go to work. It's not like some stranger came into the house and changed my painting.

Maybe Mom was right. There is definitely something strange about this painting. I just can't put my finger on it.

CHAPTER 8

LIVING LANDSCAPE

That night, I have a dream. Everything is in black and white. For some reason, my dreams are always like this.

I'm at an easel in a white room. The walls seem to go on forever.

My painting of the girl on the lake is in front of me. It's almost complete.

As I move the brush across the canvas, I feel good. Another painting is almost done! There's nothing like that feeling for me. Getting something that was in my head on a canvas is the best. After finishing a painting, I usually take a week off. Then I start a new one.

While working, I notice something. The sky on the canvas seems to be shrinking.

I continue painting, trying to fill in the sky. Then I realize the whole canvas is getting smaller.

Maybe I just need to finish this? I think in the dream. *Then the canvas will stop shrinking?*

My brush moves furiously. The canvas gets smaller

and smaller. Somehow, I've got to get this painting done before it disappears completely.

I'm working too fast. All the colors get mixed up. It's hard to tell what's on the canvas. In the dream, my painting looks gray. The canvas continues to shrink. Eventually, it disappears.

Light shines through the endless white room. The four walls surrounding me disappear.

All of a sudden, I'm standing in my painting!

From the lakeshore, I see the girl in the rowboat. She hangs over the side. Her arm dangles in the water. The bright sun shines down on her. I look over and see the tiny cabin.

"Hey!" I call to the girl in the boat.

There's no response.

"*Hey!*" I call louder.

The girl pulls her arm out of the lake and looks up at me. Her face has no eyes or nose. There are just black sockets where they should be. She looks like the man in the Ophelia Wretch painting.

I can't look at her. When I turn away, the orange man is behind me. His shadow is long and dark.

He glares down at me with his full face. The man has a big, ruddy nose. His eyes are black. They seem dead.

"Welcome!" he says in a gruff voice.

CHAPTER 9

BUMP IN THE NIGHT

Suddenly, my eyes pop open. The room is dark and quiet. My heart is pounding.

Once my eyes adjust, I make sure this is my bedroom. It is. That's a relief.

What about my painting, though? I want to look over at it, but I'm too scared. Will it look the same? Or will it look like it did in my dream?

For a moment, I lie still. The dream begins to fade. It's silly to think any of it was real. I'm sure the painting is just like it was when I fell asleep.

Slowly, I look over at it. Moonlight shines in through the window. It casts a dim light on the canvas.

My painting looks fine. The girl is still in the boat. Her arm dangles in the water. She looks down, so her face isn't visible. It's exactly how I left it.

Then I glance at the orange man. It looks like he may have shifted again. Eyes or no eyes, he seems to be looking directly at me.

Quickly, I pull the covers over my head. Am I losing my mind? What is happening?

Thankfully, my phone is on the nightstand. Staying under the covers, I reach my hand out and grab it. First, I check the time. It's almost 2 a.m.

My next thought is to text Steven and Kendra. Then I realize that's a bad idea. For one thing, they're probably asleep. For another, they will think I'm crazy. Nobody will believe a man in a painting is staring at me. Even if they did, how could they help me?

Maybe I should text my parents. What would I say, though? *My painting is scaring me! Help!* Somehow, I don't think they would take that seriously.

I decide to go to their room. There's just the little matter of getting out from under the covers.

My imagination is running wild. What if the orange man is somehow out of the painting? He could be hovering over the bed now!

Thinking like this is not helping me. I take a deep breath. Then I pull the covers off and bolt out of my room.

My parents always leave the hallway light on. They started doing it when we were kids in case we got up in the middle of the night. Luckily, it's a habit they never broke. Tonight I need the light more than ever.

I sprint past Doug's room. His door is closed. A picture of Bob Ross hangs on it. Doug put it there to make fun of me. Bob Ross's paintings are cool, in my opinion. My brother and his friends think he's funny. Right now, there's nothing funny to me about painting at all.

I reach the door to my parents' bedroom. Slowly, I turn the knob. The door creaks open. Light from the hallway streams into the dark room.

Mom turns over in bed. I stop moving, trying to be as quiet as possible. She remains asleep. Dad does too.

Gently, I shut the door and walk over by their bed. I lie down on the floor.

The carpet isn't comfortable at all. I didn't think to bring any pillows or blankets. Still, this is better than being alone in my room. At least there are no creepy paintings to give me nightmares here.

I close my eyes. If I can just get back to sleep, everything will be fine. In a few hours, the sun will come up. Then this crazy night will be over.

In the dark, I hear my parents breathing. I try to concentrate on that. Hopefully this will help me fall asleep faster.

Then a noise makes me jump.

It sounds like someone stomping hard.

Stomp!

Stomp!

Stomp!

Is that Doug? Why is he walking around the house this late?

The stomping continues. It doesn't sound like Doug. He gets up in the night sometimes. Even with his big feet, though, he doesn't make stomping sounds.

The sound seems to be moving away. I think it's going downstairs.

Then I hear something else. It's a creaking noise. Someone is opening the front door. A second later, it slams shut.

I expect my parents to wake up for sure. They don't.

Maybe Doug will wake up. I hold my breath and listen for his footsteps.

Nothing happens. The house is silent.

It seems I'm the only one who heard anything. I have no idea who or what left my house.

I don't think I want to know.

CHAPTER 10

NO EASY ANSWERS

The next morning, my family is sitting at the kitchen table. There's a bowl of cereal in front of me. I don't feel like eating though.

"We had a late-night visitor," Dad says. "That was a surprise."

He sips his coffee and reads the news on his tablet. Dad is an English professor at Scarecrow College. This means he's almost always reading something. Today he's dressed in a brown corduroy jacket, a blue button-down shirt, and jeans. It's definitely the look of an English professor.

Mom sits across from him. She's wearing a black pantsuit. As a financial planner at Scarecrow Bank, she doesn't get to wear jeans to work like Dad.

"A visitor? Who?" Doug asks.

My brother scarfs down his waffles. They're the frozen kind that you put in the toaster. Mom is always trying to get him to make them from scratch.

Doug never wants to. He says it's too much work.

"Your sister," Mom says.

She sips her coffee and eyes my dad. Then they both look at me.

"I just wanted to sleep in your room," I say. "It has been a while since I did that."

My body is stiff all over. Sleeping on the floor was no fun. The ground was cold and hard. It was a miserable experience. Still, it was better than being watched by the orange man.

"You did *what*?" Doug says loudly. "Why would you sleep in Mom and Dad's room? Did you wet the bed?" He cracks up.

Now I'm really regretting last night.

"Shut up," I say. "You were the one stomping around the house last night. Thanks for waking me up with your big feet!"

Doug hates when people talk about his feet. He wears a size 13 shoe. His basketball shoes make his feet look even bigger.

"What are you talking about?"

"You stomped all over the house. Then you went outside."

"No way. I didn't get up at all last night, liar."

I stare down at my bowl of cereal. Is my brother

lying? Doug usually doesn't lie about stuff like that. There's no reason for him to. We share a bathroom. It's between our rooms. He could have just said he got up to use it. But he doesn't say that.

If it wasn't Doug stomping around last night, who was it?

After breakfast, I need to get dressed for school. There's only one problem. My clothes are in my room. I haven't been in there this morning.

Eventually, I'll have to go back in my room. My parents won't let me sleep on their floor forever. But I'm not excited about seeing the orange man. Maybe I can grab my clothes without looking at him.

I dash into my room and grab jeans, a T-shirt, and my favorite black sweater. Then I dart into the bathroom. There's no way I'm changing in my room today.

After getting dressed and brushing my long, black hair, I head downstairs. Then something stops me short. My backpack is still in my room.

Sighing, I turn around and go back upstairs. In the bedroom, my eyes stay glued to the floor. *Don't look at the painting*, I think. My backpack is on the floor by the bed. I sling it over my shoulder and run out of the room.

CHAPTER 11

HERE'S LOOKIN' AT YOU, KID

Thankfully, the school day is normal. Steven, Kendra, and I hang out before first period. I don't mention any of the weird things that are happening. At break, we watch a silly cat video on Kendra's phone. My friends are a good distraction. For most of the morning, I forget about the orange man.

During fourth period, I have history. Mr. Morales talks about the first colonies in the U.S.

"The early settlers had to develop systems," Mr. Morales says. "Systems of commerce, trade, housing, and so on. Imagine coming to a new land and not having those things. Think about having to start from scratch."

The textbook is on our tablets. I scroll around and look at the pictures. This is what I always do before I read. It helps me understand what I'm studying better.

Looking at the pictures, I notice something. The

subjects seem to be watching me. Their eyes follow my gaze. It's not just their eyes either. Their heads seem to move as well.

Oh no, I think. *This can't be happening.*

I squeeze my eyes shut. At first it was just paintings. Now it's happening with pictures too. Why am I the only person who sees it?

Slowly, I open my eyes again. Then I examine the pictures more closely. The subjects seem to adjust themselves. It's like they know someone is watching them.

"Tabitha," Mr. Morales says. "Earth to Tabitha."

His voice startles me. I wonder how long he has been calling my name. A bunch of my classmates are laughing. Raphael laughs the loudest.

"What were some difficulties the early settlers faced?"

"Um," I say, trying to remember what I read before the pictures started moving. "Not having cars?"

My classmates laugh even harder.

Mr. Morales smiles. "That wouldn't be something Americans would think about until the early 1900s." He looks around the room. "Who wants to help Tabitha out?"

Of course, Raphael raises his hand.

"They didn't have places to live when they came here," he says confidently. "There were no systems like trade or commerce in place."

"Very good," Mr. Morales says. He continues talking about the colonists. Raphael gives me a know-it-all smile.

Now I'm embarrassed. Instead of following along on my tablet, I just listen to Mr. Morales. The last thing I want to do is look at those pictures again.

CHAPTER 12

PICTURES ALIVE

I'm sitting in art class when Raphael walks up to me.

"You're welcome," he says.

"For what?"

After what happened in history, I don't want to talk to him. All I want to do is get sixth period over with and go home.

"I figured you'd want to thank me for helping you out in history," Raphael says. "You need to pay more attention in class, Tabitha. That's the problem with your paintings too. No attention to detail."

My jaw drops. Is Raphael giving me painting advice? It takes everything I have not to scream.

"Okay," I say, still staring at my computer. Right now I'm working with castles and other inanimate objects. Luckily, they can't look back at me. As long as I focus on my work, the rest of the day should go smoothly.

This lasts for about five minutes. That's when

45

I notice something. The images on the walls of Mr. Zamora's room are looking at me now.

Art students have hung up photos on the classroom walls. They take pictures and then edit them in photo apps. People might put their friends on the moon. Some insert themselves into photos with celebrities.

I've seen these images all semester. Now they're different though. Every eye seems to be on me.

The discovery rattles me so much I mess up my *Clan Castles* poster. First, the yellow titles get turned pink. I'm able to fix them quickly, but my hands are shaking. After clicking somewhere on accident, a cyclops appears on my poster. It stares at me with its one huge eye.

Now I'm almost in a full-blown panic. *Class will be over soon*, I repeat to myself. Taking deep breaths also helps.

"What are you doing, Tabitha?" Raphael asks. "Why aren't you working?"

I look up at him. He's smiling at me. His smile isn't friendly though. It's like I'm a painting and he can see my flaws. Raphael knows there's something wrong with me.

"I *am* working."

Then I pull out my phone. Maybe taking a video

will prove that these pictures are looking at me. People are always taking pictures in art class. Nobody will think it's weird.

My hands shake as I try to open the camera app. The photo album pops open instead. This instantly takes me to a picture of the orange man. It's the one I posted on Instagram.

I gasp. The photo of the orange man has changed too. His skin is no longer orange at all. The colors of the painting look rich and fresh. There are eyes instead of black sockets now. Somehow, the man's nose is just about finished.

Then the picture changes before my eyes. The man in the painting scowls. His scowl turns into evil laughter. He has big, yellow teeth.

"Ahhhh!" I yell. "A picture can't do this!"

Everybody in the class looks at me now.

"Tabitha," Mr. Zamora says, walking over. "Are you okay?"

My face is hot with embarrassment. "I'm fine," I say quietly. "Just . . . super excited about my poster."

"That's great. Please just keep it down a little so everybody can work."

"I will."

For the rest of the period, no work gets done. It

takes all my energy to act normal even though I'm horrified inside.

Raphael keeps looking at me, but I ignore him. Every so often, he giggles. The fact that he thinks this is funny upsets me even more. He has no idea what I'm going through. How can I work on art when all the art in the world seems to be haunting me?

CHAPTER 13

ART IMITATING LIFE

After school, I run home. Even though the painting of the orange man is there, it still seems safer than school. I need some quiet time alone. Somehow I've got to figure out what's going on.

I burst into the house. Nobody's home. My parents are both at work. Doug is at basketball practice.

Once I'm inside, the paintings and pictures on the walls seem overwhelming. There are so many. Looking at them feels risky. I stare straight ahead on the way up to my room.

At this point, I don't have a plan. I just need to get over my fear and look at the painting of the orange man. Maybe all of this is in my head. Paintings don't come to life. My mind has probably been playing tricks on me.

I take a deep breath and walk into my room. After tossing my backpack to the ground, I look at the painting.

The orange man isn't in it anymore.

"What?" I scream. "How . . .? Where . . .?"

I can't form a sentence.

Maybe this wasn't all in my head after all.

I pull out my phone and start to call my parents. But they're both still at work. If I tell them what's happening, they're going to think I'm crazy. Everybody at school probably already thinks that.

For a moment, I stare at the dark, empty canvas of the Ophelia Wretch painting. It's amazing how the orange man has completely disappeared from it. There's an outline where his body was, but it looks like nothing was ever there.

I've got to take a picture of this. The empty canvas is proof nobody will be able to argue with.

I lift up my phone and am about to open the camera. Then the phone vibrates and my screen changes. Steven and Kendra want to video chat. Before I realize what's happening, I've swiped to answer it.

"Hey!" they say together. It looks like they're walking down the street.

"Hi."

I try not to sound too nervous. It's hard because I'm completely freaking out.

"Do you want to go to the mall?" Steven asks.

"We wanted to ask you after school," Kendra says.

"But we didn't see you."

"And you didn't respond to any of our texts," Steven adds.

The mall sounds great. I'll be out of the house with my friends. That will definitely be better than staying home alone with paintings and pictures that are alive.

"Sure!" I chirp.

Then I practically run out of my house. The painting can wait.

Luckily, the mall is within walking distance. When I get there, Steven and Kendra are waiting for me. It's a relief to be with my friends. We walk around together.

Within a few minutes, though, it starts happening again. Every poster on the wall and every image I see is looking at me.

In Shawn's Super Retro Arcade, all the video game characters glare at me. I tell Steven and Tabitha I'm hungry just so we can leave.

The food court is no better. There are huge pictures on the walls. They show people eating pizza and hot dogs. All of them seem to be staring at me too. I focus on my French fries to keep myself from panicking.

"Tabitha," Steven says. "What's wrong?"

"Nothing." I take a sip of my soda. My eyes stay focused on the table.

"Tab," Kendra laughs. "What's going on? You just drank my soda."

Steven and Kendra crack up. I smile and pretend to laugh. This will make them think everything is fine. They know I sometimes do quirky things like this.

"Sorry about that," I say to Kendra. Then I take another sip of her drink.

We all laugh harder.

"Are you nervous about the art show on Saturday?" Kendra asks.

Somehow I completely forgot about the art show. I've been too busy being scared. Now my mind fills with new worries. How am I going to deal with all the paintings at the show? What if they all look at me?

Before my mind goes too far down that rabbit hole, something catches my eye from across the food court.

It's the orange man.

Not only is he fully painted, but he's also *alive*. The orange man looks completely human. People walk past him like anybody else. Nobody thinks it's odd that he's here.

Fear paralyzes me. I can't say anything to my friends. There's no way to explain that the creepy subject of my Ophelia Wretch painting came to life and followed me to the mall. Who would believe that?

If I wasn't seeing it with my own eyes, I wouldn't.

I continue to stare at the orange man. Why is he here? What does he want?

Finally, the man scowls at me and walks away.

Without thinking, I spring up and run after him.

"Tabitha!" Steven and Kendra call. "Where are you going?"

There's no time to tell them. I've got to talk to the orange man. Suddenly, I'm certain that only he can explain what's going on.

I chase after him in the sea of mall shoppers. My legs are moving as fast as they can. For someone who isn't even real, the orange man sure moves fast.

For several minutes, I'm able to keep my eyes on him. Then he turns a corner. I break into a full run to try to catch up.

When I get around the corner, my heart sinks. There are sliding glass doors that lead to the parking lot. The sun is going down. It's early evening.

The orange man is gone.

CHAPTER 14

BACK AND GONE AGAIN

I bolt from the mall without telling my friends.

My phone vibrates in my pocket. Steven and Kendra are texting me.

Steven

where r u?

Kendra

r u ok?

I don't want them to worry, but all I can think about right now is the orange man. There's no way I can go back in the mall. Too many pictures were looking at me.

Tabitha

my mom texted.
she wants me home. sorry!

Mom probably isn't home from work yet. My friends don't know that though. Hopefully they believe my excuse.

As I walk through the mall parking lot, I'm on high alert. There are no signs of the orange man anywhere. He seems to have vanished.

The sky is getting darker. Rain clouds are moving in. My house seems like the only place to go. Will the orange man be waiting for me there?

I rush home before it starts pouring.

None of the lights are on in the house. It doesn't look like anyone is home yet. For once, I actually wish my brother were here. If the orange man wanted to attack me, my brother's giant feet could stop him.

I take a deep breath and unlock the door.

Everything seems normal. The house looks just like it did when I left.

After turning some lights on, I decide to go up to my room. I'm scared, but I've got to see the Ophelia Wretch painting again. Surely I imagined what happened earlier. How could the orange man be walking around outside the canvas?

My feet carry me up the stairs slowly.

I open my bedroom door and flick the light on. Then I look at the painting.

The orange man is back in it!

Now the painting looks exactly how it did when I got it. Once again, the man's skin is orange. His nose and eye sockets are black. He doesn't seem to be staring at me anymore.

I pull out my phone. Has the picture I took of the painting changed back too? In art class, the painting looked fresh. The orange man was alive. He laughed at me.

Somehow, the picture on my phone is back to normal too. It looks just like it did when I originally posted it online.

Now I really have no idea what's going on.

A noise startles me.

"Tabitha? Are you home?"

It's my mom. I rush downstairs, shutting my bedroom door behind me. This is the happiest I've ever been to hear my parents come home.

For the rest of the evening, I try not to think about the orange man. We eat dinner. Then Doug goes upstairs to do homework. I do all mine at the kitchen table.

At bedtime, my parents go up to their room. A few minutes later, I follow them. I grab my pajamas, pillow, and blanket out of my room. The painting of the orange man seems normal. Still, I can't chance sleeping in here tonight. What if he walks out of the painting again?

I change in the bathroom and then check to see if the light in my parents' room is off. It is. Quietly, I open the door.

"Honey," Mom says. She and Dad are both in bed. "You have a bedroom, you know."

"Yeah," Dad says. "And it has a comfortable bed. A bed we paid a lot of money for."

They're annoyed. Of course they don't want me sleeping on their floor every night. For a second, I consider telling them the truth. What would I say?

Mom, Dad, I need to sleep in here because my Ophelia Wretch painting is alive. The orange man actually came out of it today and went to the mall.

That wouldn't go over well. Mom would probably insist on taking me to the hospital.

"Well," I say, arranging my pillow and blanket. "I *am* growing up. We should try to maximize our time together. You know, while I'm still kind of a kid."

My parents laugh. "Okay," Mom says. "Goodnight."

After everything that happened today, my body is exhausted. Within moments, I'm asleep.

A few hours later, the stomping sound wakes me up again.

Stomp.

Stomp.

Stomp.

Fear moves through every inch of my body. The orange man must be walking around again. I pull the blanket up over my head.

I want my parents to wake up. If they hear it too, maybe they'll believe me.

Then I have a new fear. What if the orange man hurts my family?

The stomping sound moves farther away. Just like last night, I hear the front door open and close.

I lie in the darkness of my parents' bedroom, shaking. For a long time, I listen for strange noises. The house stays quiet though. Eventually, I fall asleep.

CHAPTER 15

STOLEN

The next morning, I walk into the kitchen. My dad is at the table. He's sipping orange juice as he reads the news on his tablet.

"Hi, honey. Did you sleep okay?" he asks.

Mom and Doug are upstairs getting dressed. Maybe I should tell Dad about the orange man. He says I can always come to him for advice.

"Yeah," I say. "It was better with the blanket and pillow." The truth is that I'm tired. My body is stiff.

"I'll bet."

I pour a bowl of cereal and try to eat. My stomach is doing flip-flops. All I can think about is the orange man.

"Oh, no!" Dad says. He turns his tablet toward me. "All three Ophelia Wretch paintings were stolen from the Scarecrow Library."

"What?"

"Yeah. This article says somebody took them last night."

"Did they take any other paintings?"

"It doesn't say. Who would do that?"

I have an idea. It's not something I can share with my dad though.

"Better get ready for school!" I quickly stand up.

"You hardly ate any breakfast," Dad says.

"It's okay. I'm not hungry."

Outside my bedroom door, I take a deep breath. Slowly, I step in the room.

My eyes turn to the wall with the painting on it. The orange man is there. But he looks different than last night. Once again, his paint looks fresh. His eyes are no longer just black sockets. They're real eyes now. His nose is filled in too.

There's a new change. His lips are turned up in an evil grin.

I've seen enough. It takes me seconds to grab my clothes and backpack. Then I head to the bathroom, closing my bedroom door behind me.

A few minutes later, I'm dressed and back downstairs. "Bye, Mom," I call, slinging my backpack over my shoulder. "Bye, Dad."

"Bye, dear," he says.

"Have a great day," Mom calls.

I walk outside. Today seems like a normal day. There's only one difference. I'm not going to school.

CHAPTER 16

THE ENEMY

When I open the door of the Vintage Rose Antique Shop, it jingles.

Even though I haven't been here in years, the shop looks just how I remember. The place is packed with stuff. Most of it looks ancient. Random items sit on dusty shelves. There are old gadgets, paintings, books, and knickknacks.

A woman stands behind the counter. She's organizing some jewelry.

"Good morning," she says with a smile. "Shouldn't you be in school?"

The woman is right. I *should* be in school. But today there is more pressing business, like finding out why a painting is terrorizing me.

"Um, it's a late-start day," I lie.

I eye the old clock on the wall behind the counter. The time is 9:15 a.m. On late-start days, we go at 10:05 a.m. At least my excuse is believable.

"Oh," the woman says. She laughs. "That's news to me. My daughter didn't say anything about it. Do you go to Scarecrow Middle School?"

"Yes."

"Maybe you know my daughter. Her name is Tenley."

"Not really, sorry." I've heard of Tenley. She's an eighth grader, I think. But that's all I know about her.

My nose wrinkles. There's a strange smell in this shop. I can't quite place it. It's not good, though.

"So what brings you to the Vintage Rose this morning?" The woman continues organizing behind the counter.

"I was given a painting," I say. "For my birthday. My aunt said she got it here. It's of an orange man . . ."

"Oh!" the woman says. "You're the one who got that. I love that painting. The man in it is so interesting."

"Yeah, he is. I was wondering if you could tell me anything else about it?"

The woman reaches under the counter. She pulls out an old, ratty blue book.

"Let me see," she says, flipping through the pages. "This book is fairly extensive. It catalogs pretty much everything in this place. Is this it?" She holds up the blue book. There's a drawing of the Ophelia Wretch painting. It's in black and white. I nod.

"This says the painting is called *The Enemy*," the woman starts. "Ophelia Wretch was the artist. The subject is a man named Herbert Whitmore. He and Ophelia were both artists from Sunnyside. Apparently they were very competitive. They were so competitive, in fact, that when a fire broke out at one of Ophelia's art shows, Herbert was blamed. The ceiling sprinklers went off and destroyed a bunch of her paintings. After that, Herbert was shunned by the art world. Nobody wanted to work with him because of what they thought he did to Ophelia."

"Did he really start the fire?" I ask.

"According to this, Herbert always said he was innocent. Many didn't believe him though. Ophelia created the painting of him to get revenge. She took the canvas to a witch doctor and had it cursed."

"Wow," I say. My painting is cursed? That explains a lot.

The woman keeps reading. "While painting it, Ophelia found out she was sick. Doctors told her she only had six months to live. She stopped working on the painting."

"That's why Herbert's eyes and nose are missing!" I say. "Ophelia never finished it."

"Right. Ophelia felt bad about the curse. Before she

died, she wished to make peace with Herbert."

"Did she ever tell him she forgave him?"

"No. She died before the curse could be lifted. Then Herbert died a few years later. They say he was bitter and penniless. He never forgave Ophelia for ruining his art career. Up until his death, Herbert swore that he would get revenge."

CHAPTER 17

PEACE OFFERING

The woman at the Vintage Rose gave me so much to think about. After leaving the store, I walk slowly down the street. My mind is swirling. All I want to do is sit down.

Scarecrow Park is nearby. It has a playground and benches. Since it's still early and the sky is overcast, nobody is there. I find a dry bench and pull out my phone.

It feels silly, but I Google "lifting a curse." The search results only confuse me more. There are websites about witchcraft. Some mention black magic. A few have recipes for potions. This is all too much for me to deal with.

I close my eyes. Maybe I just need to figure out what Herbert wants. Why is he coming out of the painting? What is he looking for?

Then I remember what my dad told me. Three Ophelia Wretch paintings were stolen from the library.

The orange man stomped out of the house last night.

Suddenly it hits me. Herbert is trying to get rid of Ophelia Wretch's paintings!

Maybe Herbert wants people to forget about Ophelia. He's trying to take away her career like she took his. The orange man is turning Ophelia's curse on her.

There are more than 300 Ophelia Wretch paintings in the world. The cursed one is in my room. Three others have been taken from the library. Which ones will Herbert go after next?

A sense of panic fills me. Ophelia forgave Herbert! I wish there was a way he could know that. It might be enough to stop him.

The woman at the Vintage Rose told me Herbert lived in Sunnyside.

Slowly, a plan forms in my head. I have no idea if it will work, but it's my only hope.

There's no time to waste. First, I head home to pick up a few things. Then I'm on the next bus to Sunnyside.

An hour later, the bus lets me off in a suburban neighborhood. The houses in Sunnyside look newer than most of the ones in Scarecrow. It's sunny here too. Scarecrow is almost always overcast.

I have taken the bus to visit my cousin Denise a few times, so I have an idea of where to go. The address I'm looking for is a few blocks away. Normally that would be a short walk. But today there's a large painting in my arms. It slows me down a bit.

Before leaving my house, I covered the painting of Herbert Whitmore in a blanket. One reason was to protect it. The other was to avoid looking at him. Thankfully, he didn't do anything crazy on the bus. He may have changed positions. His paint may have gotten fresher. But at least Herbert stayed in his canvas. That's good enough for me.

Directions on my phone guide me to 8396 Kibler Street. Eventually, I find myself in front of a brown one-story home.

I walk up to the front door and knock. Only now do I consider that it's the middle of the day. The people I'm looking for might not be home.

Standing there, I wonder if this is a good idea. Coming here was a split-second decision. It was surprisingly easy to find Herbert's relatives online. I used some of the birthday money my grandparents gave me to buy the bus ticket. Hopefully I can get home before anyone realizes I'm gone.

After what seems like forever, a woman answers the door. She's tall with a big nose and black hair. In a way, she looks like Herbert.

"Hello?" she says. Her eyes are curious.

"Hi," I say nervously. "Um, this might be a strange question. But are you related to Herbert Whitmore?"

"Why?" The woman's eyes narrow. She's almost scowling. Now she looks even more like Herbert.

"Because," I go on, showing her the painting. "I got this painting of him. Ophelia Wretch was the artist. It seems like she would've wanted Herbert's family to have it."

The woman takes the painting.

"Herbert was my great uncle," she says. "I know that he and Ophelia were enemies. Are you related to her?"

"No," I say. "The painting was given to me as a gift. I just thought it was something you should have. Apparently they had some issues. Ophelia wanted Herbert to know she wasn't mad at him anymore. She didn't want him to be mad at her, either. Sadly, they both died before they could work things out."

We talk for a few more minutes. The woman thanks me for the painting. She says her Uncle Herbert would be happy to know Ophelia wanted to make amends.

Walking back to the bus stop is much easier without the painting. I feel relieved. The bus should get me to Scarecrow by the time school is out. Now I'm just hoping what I did today was enough.

CHAPTER 18

THE END OF ART

When I get home, everything seems fine. The pictures on the walls no longer stare at me. Nobody seems to have noticed I missed school.

Maybe the curse between Herbert and Ophelia is actually broken. I imagine the two of them hanging out in the afterlife. Perhaps they're painting something together.

For the first time in days, I sleep in my room. My parents are relieved. No stomping sounds wake me up in the night. In the morning, I actually feel rested.

At school, there's a test in history class. Sadly, I forgot to study for it. Missing school yesterday put me behind. My whole week has been thrown off by Herbert Whitmore. At least things seem to be going back to normal now.

I do my best on the test. Afterward, Mr. Morales gives us free time. We're supposed to work on homework from other classes.

"Where were you yesterday?" Donovan asks. He sits by me in history. "You never miss."

"I was sick," I lie.

He reminds me about my unexcused absence. I've got to figure out how to clear it. Personally, I think lifting a curse is a good reason to miss school. Principal Legend might not agree though.

As I scroll around on my tablet, a headline catches my eye:

"Stolen Wretch Paintings Vandalized and Returned"

A photo shows the three Ophelia Wretch paintings taken from the Scarecrow Library. The subjects are gone from all of them.

My body starts to shake. This looks like the work of the orange man. What if giving the painting to Herbert's family didn't change anything?

For the rest of the day, I can't focus. If Herbert is still out to destroy Ophelia's paintings, I have to stop him. But how?

Later that night, I sit downstairs with my parents. I play *Clan Castles* on my phone to distract myself. Normally, this would be painting time. My mind can't focus on that right now though.

Dad turns on the evening news.

"Wow," he says. "Art thefts are happening nationwide."

I look up at the TV. A reporter is standing in front of a museum. "According to police, this is the fifteenth museum to be vandalized," she says. "In each case, paintings were stolen. The subjects were somehow removed. Then the paintings were returned to the museums."

As she talks, they show the paintings. All of them are missing the main subject. It looks like somebody photo-edited them. But these are canvases, not digital photos.

My jaw drops. How can Herbert be doing this? The museums are all over the world. There's no way he could get to them so quickly. Unless . . .

"He's not working alone," I whisper aloud.

"What?" Dad asks.

"Oh, nothing."

"Is everything okay?" Mom asks.

"Yeah," I mumble.

It looks like Herbert is getting help from the subjects in the other paintings. He takes one out. Then they take other subjects out. This must be why it's happening all over the world.

Maybe Herbert isn't just after Ophelia's paintings

anymore. Everyone turned against him. He probably wants revenge on the whole art world.

What if they take every subject out of every painting ever made? Then no more paintings will exist. It won't just be Ophelia's legacy that's forgotten. It will be everyone's!

I quickly race upstairs. When I walk into my bedroom, I'm stunned.

The girl in the boat is gone from my painting.

CHAPTER 19

ART SHOW RIOT

The next day is Saturday. My parents and I go to the art show. Doug even comes along. "I just want to laugh at how bad all the paintings are," he says.

I'm too nervous to care. The news is not good. Subjects are still disappearing from paintings. There doesn't seem to be an end in sight.

The art show is in the middle of the library. As we walk in, I see that the organizers have done an awesome job. All the paintings are on display. Thankfully, the subjects are still in them. There are even easels and canvases set up so people can create their own paintings.

Everybody is dressed up. I see some of my classmates with their families. Members of the library's board of trustees walk around. They're judging the entries.

While looking for my painting, we run into Steven and Kendra.

"Are you excited?" Steven asks. "Your painting could hang in here *forever!*"

"You're going to be so famous one day," Kendra says. My friends smile at me.

I smile back. Part of me wants to tell them what I think is happening. Herbert could come any minute and take the cowgirl out of my painting. Soon, all paintings might cease to exist. Even if they believed me, though, what could we do?

"Oh, there it is!" Mom has spotted my painting. She makes a beeline for it. Dad and I follow her. That's when I notice that my painting is right next to Raphael's. He's standing in front of his with his parents.

I think about Ophelia and Herbert's rivalry. Are we like them? No. As much as he bothers me at times, I don't dislike Raphael. I'd never want anything bad to happen to him or his paintings.

A loud noise breaks my train of thought.

"Oh no," I whisper.

People get quiet and look around. The sound gets louder and louder.

Stomp.

Stomp.

Stomp.

Herbert appears. He isn't alone. *Man on a Bridge*, *Girl in the City*, and *Sailor at Sea* are with him. They are all subjects from Ophelia's paintings. Each scowls like Herbert.

Also with them is the girl from my painting. Since I never painted her face, she doesn't have one.

"Let the art liberation begin!" Herbert cries.

Herbert and his gang start touching the paintings. Instantly, the subjects jump out of them.

People scream as the paintings come to life. My cowgirl rides around the library on her horse. The bride from Raphael's painting rips books off the shelves. Both of them touch other paintings too. More subjects leap out.

Soon the library is in pandemonium. Some of the subjects open books. They start touching the pictures in them. Even more subjects come out of them. I see the *Mona Lisa*, Abraham Lincoln, and Martin Luther King Jr. running around.

"Tabitha!" Kendra cries. She runs over to me, holding up her phone. Her news app is open. "This is happening *all over the world!*"

Steven follows her. "I just opened Instagram!" he shouts. "All the subjects are leaving our pictures!"

"If this keeps up, there won't be any more pictures, paintings, or anything," Doug cries.

"And it's going to be all *your* fault, Tabitha!" Raphael screams. He runs up behind us. The bride from his painting is chasing him. "*You* unleashed that weird orange man on the world!"

"No! I tried to stop him!"

"Stop *me?*" Herbert cries. He lets out an evil laugh. Everyone can see his big, gross, yellow teeth. "You'll never stop *real* art!"

CHAPTER 20

REAL COLLABORATION

The art show is pure chaos. Nobody knows what to do. People hide under tables. Some try to force the subjects back into their pictures. Nothing is working though.

Suddenly, I get an idea. It's a long shot but it might work.

I run over to the easels and start painting.

"What are you doing?" Dad shouts.

"Art got us into this mess," I say. "Maybe art can get us out of it!"

Using black paint, I make the outlines of Ophelia and Herbert.

"Tabitha," Raphael snaps. "Now is not the time to be painting!"

"Now is the *best* time! Come on!" I say, grabbing him by the hand. "Everybody start painting! We've all got to work together."

Steven and Kendra grab brushes. They start painting at other easels.

I hand Raphael a paintbrush. "Will you help me? I need someone to fill in my outlines."

At first, he stares at me like I'm nuts. Then he grabs the brush and starts painting. I smile at him before rushing off to pass out more brushes and canvases.

Other students from our class start painting as well. People are making art left and right.

"Stop this!" Herbert cries. "Stop it at once! If I can't have a painting career, nobody can!"

He scowls as we continue to paint.

Parents and teachers join in. My brother does too. Some of the subjects even start painting. The chaos calms down. People focus on their creations.

I help Raphael finish the painting of Herbert and Ophelia. We add mountains to the background. The subjects are smiling at each other. For a quick piece, I think we've done a pretty good job.

Then Herbert comes up behind us. He sees the painting of him and Ophelia.

Slowly, his scowl softens. A tear runs down his cheek.

"You know, Ophelia was my friend once," he says quietly. More tears run down his face. "We were competitive too. But I would never do anything to hurt her."

"So you didn't start the fire?" I ask gently. "You didn't ruin Ophelia's paintings?"

"Heavens, no!" Herbert says. "But everyone blamed me. No one would display my art anywhere. So I stopped painting. My anger at Ophelia for taking away my career was too great."

"Ophelia regretted what happened too," I tell him. "She cursed you in her painting. But she wanted to lift the curse. Sadly, she died before it could happen."

Herbert looks at me with sad eyes. "Knowing that would've been enough. I could have moved on. My bitterness kept me here. It made me come out of her painting. Revenge was all I could think about. I tried to destroy art . . . the very thing I love."

Herbert continues to stare at the painting of him and Ophelia.

"But seeing all of you . . . you love art so much. You're inspired by our paintings. All of you are working together to save art!"

"Herbert," I say, smiling. "You can help us save art too."

He smiles back at me. Then he turns to all the other subjects.

"We must go back to our canvases at once!" Herbert shouts. "So that art can live on forever!"

In an instant, all the subjects return to their paintings and pictures. Aside from the library being a mess, it's like they were never here.

People crawl out from their hiding spots. Kendra checks her phone.

"All the paintings around the world are going back to normal too!" she cries.

"Well," one library trustee says. "I think we all know which painting deserves to win this competition."

He points to the picture of Ophelia and Herbert. Another trustee puts a blue ribbon on it.

"A true collaboration saved the world of art," I say.

Everybody cheers.

After the cheering dies down, we clean up the library. Soon all the books are back on the shelves. Tables and chairs are lined up. The paintings hang neatly on the walls again.

"Well," Raphael says, smiling. "I guess we *both* won the art show."

I grin. "That's right."

"Sorry for what I said earlier," he goes on. "I didn't really think all this was your fault. It's just that you're such a good artist. Sometimes I'm jealous."

"Raphael, you're a great artist too. I think we could learn a lot from each other."

"You do?"

"Yeah. Do you want to work on another collaboration sometime?"

"Definitely," he says. "Just one thing. Next time, can we plan it in advance? I work better without being chased by the subject of my painting."

"Deal!" We both laugh while shaking on it.

VINTAGE ROSE
MYSTERIES

THE SECRET ROOM
978-1-68021-758-2

LUCKY ME
978-1-68021-759-9

VCR FROM BEYOND
978-1-68021-760-5

NEW PAINTING
978-1-68021-761-2

CALL WAITING
978-1-68021-762-9

WWW.SDLBACK.COM/VINTAGE-ROSE-MYSTERIES